Coffee and Dreams

Volume 2

Coffee and Dreams

Volume: 2

Short stories with

JJ Caler

Introducing

Daniel Nick

Published by JJ Caler Publishing

Coffee and Dreams

Volume 2

First publication, August, 2024

Copyright © 2024 J.J. Caler

The Ace of Cups

Copyright © 2024 J.J. Caler

Written by J.J. Caler

All rights reserved.

Café Muse

Copyright © 2024 Daniel Nick

Written by Daniel Nick

All rights reserved.

Dedication

Thank you, Virginia, for being our biggest fan.

Thank you, J Lee, for being our loyal reader.

JJ Caler

Thank you, Beth, for being everything real in my universe. I don't need anything else, not even coffee.

Daniel Nick

Café Muse

By Daniel Nick

Published by JJ Caler Publishing

A Short Story by
Daniel Nick

CAFE'
MUSE

Café Muse

Every morning the door opens outward and the smell - oh the blissful smell - of fresh brewed coffee comes swirling out to caress my nose with that glorious

Café Muse

olfactory sensation. If you have ever been to Cafe Muse, you know exactly what I'm talking about.

I walk in and simultaneously feel my senses come alive and my concerns melt away. All is right in the world. There's a balance to the Cafe. Harmonious.

The woman behind the counter (her name is Amelia) smiles at me and mouths the words, "The regular?".

I nod in the affirmative, hold my finger up in the sign for Menu Item Number 1 (black coffee), and walk unhurriedly to my favorite table which sits open this morning. I make sure I spread a bunch of nods around to the regulars while I walk the short, infinite distance to the table.

A nod for the exhausted Vampire, Dave, fresh off his shift

as a dispatch officer for the local community college police force. He's trying Almond milk again in his Number 47; the Cappuccino. Poor bastard.

A nod to the four otters disguised as a man in a trench coat, rearranging the four shots of espresso (four Number 4's - ha!) on the table in front of them.

A nod to the beautiful lara named Cassie, a mermaid from Brazil, who simply adores the medium roast coffee here. Splash of cream, one sugar - the Number 32.

I'm more of a dark roast man, myself.

And finally a nod to the Woman In Red, who always sits at the table off to my right, sipping her double latte - Number 87 - with both hands wrapped around the cup while staring at the pitch-black void outside her window: her eight tentacles, each exiting the dress and ending in a blood red slipper, nervously tapping on the floor in a faint, barely audible dance across the tiles. Waiting for her lover to come and destroy all the worlds in her universe, no doubt.

Outside *my* window, the early morning sun playfully casts shadows of varying angles across the geometric landscape of the city streets in a world I've never been to, but plan on visiting today. I wait for Amelia to arrive at my table with the porcelain mug of Ethiopian dark roast, and when she does, she nervously sets the mug down and says a timid, "Hi, Donald."

"Hello, Amelia," I respond slowly and quietly, trying not to spook her.

"How is your morning going? Everything okay?"

Still glacial in my speed, I reply, "It's going great now that I'm here. Thank you for the coffee, Amelia, you're an angel."

She grins, relieved. "My pleasure, Donald. Just wave when you're ready for a refill."

"Will do."

She wipes her hands on her apron and after the briefest of hesitations where I thought she might actually say more for once, she turns and walks away, down the brief, eternal length of the cafe.

I dream that one day she'll tell me if my guess is correct, but until then, I'm calling her angel no matter the truth.   I just can't imagine anything that gorgeously skittish being anything else.

The cafe is simply marvelous;   comforting   and exciting to the soul. Almost two thousand menu items, all of which are coffee or tea, and counting. I've been coming here to get my morning Joe for just about forever, and the thing I love so much about it is the absolute dependability of it all.   It's consistent.   Randomly   and chaotically so. That is to say, it's so metaphorical, that you can depend on it to be nothing like you've planned for, which is just tremendously reliable.

Still, it is somewhat of a shock to look up into the eyes of a stranger sitting across from me at my own favorite table, which is exactly what I do right now.

They smile at me and take out a tube of lipstick from their coat pocket, meticulously applying it while I stare.

"Would you like to try some?" they ask. " Ruby Red. My favorite color."

"Clashes with my boots," I reply truthfully. I find it's always better to tell as much truth as I can. Reality hates trying to keep up with lies. Causes all sorts of grumpy Déjà vu episodes. And indigestion, of course. "Who are you?"

"I am really glad to have finally found you," they say.

"That's more of a 'what are you', but I'll take it, I guess."

Café Muse

Amelia comes over to the table from across the Great Divide and looks concerned about two people sitting where only one should be. The symmetry of the entire cafe is wrong now, and even the otters are feeling it. The harmony of the Cafe has been damaged.

Looking from the stranger to me and then back again - twice - Amelia finally grips the hem of her apron with both hands and asks the stranger, "Can I get you something?"

They keep me pinned with their stare as they answer Amelia with a single word of doom.

"Decaf."

The place goes dead silent. Not the contented, peaceful silence of a house in the hour before the kids come crashing down the stairs to open their Christmas presents. No, we're talking the other kind of silence. The kind where a billion voices are screaming into the void, muted, unheard, and unsaved, as limitless horror crashes down into their souls.

I shiver.

The bastard across from me smiles.

A pot of coffee crashes to the floor of the Cafe and shatters. A thing that has never once happened here in its entirety of existence. Hell, it never even happened when it didn't exist!

Amelia opens her mouth to speak but she can't make anything come out. She is terrified. Frozen. And I can actually see a part of her shrivel up and die as the light behind her

Café Muse

beautiful green eyes dims and fails to flare back up.

For that reason alone, I want to hurt this cruel creature imposing itself into my reality.

"They do not serve that kind here." I snarl. "Everything here is real."

They reach out languidly as they sit back in an insolent slouch, their fingers cruelly running up the back of Amelia's hand. She flinches, eyes wide, staring at me for help. Pleading, really.

They look at me with infuriating smugness they say, "But isn't this Cafe Muse? Doesn't the sign outside say as plain as the lipstick on my face that Cafe Muse is 'where inspiration becomes real'?"

It did, of course. It says that proudly and truly. Cafe Muse is the comfy little infinite space between waveform observation and waveform collapse. It's also my favorite coffee shop (it can totally be both, and you know it), and that's what is so unforgivable about this assault on our morning routine.

"So what?" I reply, rather unimaginatively.

"Well, I have recently been inspired," they answer. "I've had a moment of enlightenment, and epiphany of negation, if you will."

"Negation?"

"Surely you, Donald, have guessed who I am by now?"

I sit very still, squirming mightily only on the inside. I feel I really should know them, but I...don't. This scares me more than a baby T-Rex. Which I find to be the most terrifying thing smaller than an Eldritch God. Trust me on this. Baby T-Rex's are fucking nightmares.

Their eyebrows raise incrementally for about twenty seconds until they threaten to exit their head and fall off-stage and out of the still, silent scene.

"You really haven't figured it out? I said *Decaf* for goodness sake!"

Then the answer appears in my head full grown and all Athena-like, screaming at me to run.

Decaf.

Negation.

Nameless.

"It's really you?" I state as a question. It's a last-ditch attempt to pretend it isn't them, of course. A more honest response would have been the statement, "It's really you."

I feel the indigestion kick in.

They smile at me, an innocent wickedness so pure my emotions hit absolute zero.

"Oh yes, it's me. And I think this little cafe might be just the thing."

I dread the answer but I can hear myself asking anyway, "The thing for what?"

"Why, the thing for figuring out how to turn off the universe, of course."

"Which universe?"

Café Muse

"Don't be obtuse, or even acute. All of them. Every universe, all reality, all time. Turned off. Finally."

"According to legend, you've been trying to end reality for eternity, what makes you think you can do it here and now?"

"You, Donald."

"Me?"

"You. And Decaf, of course."

"I don't understand."

"You don't need to."

"Now you're just being needlessly accurate."

They sigh theatrically and continue, "You, Donald are nothing but a man, as far as I can tell. How in creation are you even here?"

I sit quietly and slowly begin a long process of tiny incremental movements of my left hand toward the table edge. I need to get close to my jacket pocket.

They stare at my hand and I cease its movement.

"I don't know why I'm here. I just am."

"I'll tell you how you are here, Donald. Because you walk the realities of the universe the way other humans walk down the streets of your New York - totally lost and stumbling across exciting new experiences."

"Yeeesssss..." I draw out unexpectedly long.

"And you do it because this cafe makes it possible." And they point out the window to the city street of a world that existed solely in my imagination until I sat down at the table this morning.

My left hand begins to move again, and this time Nameless doesn't react.

"So you think, what?" I ask them, hoping for an answer.

"So I think that this Cafe can make 'unreal'...real.   Provided it's you that places the order."

I stand corrected, Nameless is by far the scariest thing smaller than an Eldritch God, mainly because they are a manifestation of something so alien we have to call them Nameless. There are no other words that come as close to explaining them.

"Spell it out, please."

"Donald, you're going to order me a Decaf. Right here. Right now."

"The hell I will."

They look up at the frozen Amelia and smile again, "You like all these folks, don't you? The aquatic mammals, the Vampire," Then he looks at me with all traces of humor gone, " The Lady in Red."

I glance over to the Lady in Red. She is staring at the tableau with rapt fascination, breathing heavily, like the entire pageant playing out in front of her is highly erotic in some way. I guess that for her it is. But that's because she has no idea of the kind of destruction They actually want.

The Lady is waiting for her Eldritch boyfriend to come lay waste to her universe, true, but that is simply the way of Eldritch Gods. They are destroyers. That's an honest part of reality. I had no problem with that. For every universe they are foiled, there's

17

one where they succeed. That's what balance means, and the universe does nothing if not strive for balance.

But Nameless. Nameless wants to undo reality itself. Not just destruction, but the negation of everything. The erasure of reality, time, and space. Decaf fucking coffee.

Not on my watch. And not before I've had my first cup of Ethiopian.

"Not the same and you know it," I reply.

"Pretty close though. Just splitting atoms, really."

"It's 'splitting hairs'."

"Is it?"

"Isn't it?"

They frown at me. "Order the Decaf."

"No."

"I'll undo everyone here."

"You can't or you already would have."

They hiss in frustration, "There's more than one way to undo things. I might not be able to undo them from reality, but I can ruin your morning!"

They reach out to Amelia and I lunge across the table to stop them, but it is a feint, a trick. While my body is in flight over the table, they put one hand on me and casually flick their fingers on the other hand towards the otters who shriek in surprise as they look down at themselves and discover they are now a man pretending to be four otters! And four shots of espresso is going to be way too much caffeine for them!

There's a shudder in the Cafe itself as if this is just a bit too much. I mean, honestly, four shots of Espresso for one man in a fur-lined trench coat? Insanity!

Everything is out of sorts as I regain my seat, thinking furiously now.

"How did you do that?"

"I didn't. You did."

"The heck I did!"

"Oh Donald, you gave me the ability to change them. All I had to do was touch you. Watch."

They flicked their fingers at Amelia. She flinches, but nothing happens.

"See? I can't change a thing in this cafe unless I'm touching you."

The Cafe shudders again as everyone looks at me with concern and even a few looks of suspicion.

" I don't understand," I say.

"Nor do I, really. But you don't come here to experience reality like all the others."

"Yes, I do."

"No, Donald, you don't. You somehow create reality. Or cause reality to be created in your image, perhaps. I honestly don't know how you do it, but you're going to order me a Decaf."

The lights in the cafe flair brighter momentarily before dimming to about half of their usual brightness and then they settle down at this reduced output. All the shadows in the building get longer and darker.

My stomach hurts.

Desperate and flailing for an escape I say, "I'll order you a tea or tisane. There are plenty of them that don't have caffeine. Hell, the Number 1098 is chicory. Caffeine free."

They laugh softly, "You know very well it isn't about caffeine. It's about...Decaf."

"There is no Decaf!" I yell.

I slam my right hand down on the table as my left drops down next to my coat pocket, "Decaf does not exist. There is no Decaf!"

They answer with just four words that shatter my resolve and break my heart, "There used to be."

I slump in my seat and stare down at the tabletop. Amelia finally finds her voice, "Donald? What is Decaf?"

The Cafe rumbles louder and the floor shakes enough that everyone notices.

"It's nothing," I try once more in desperation. My stomach flip flops and my indigestion doubles - triples - and I feel the need to retch, but I hold it back by swallowing rapidly four of five million times.

I try again, this time truthfully. "It's...an abomination. I'll not have it around me."

Dave calls over from his table, staring at me like I'm a beast out of his nightmares, "It's a coffee drink? But...We have every coffee drink in the universe here. Look at the menu..."

They interrupt, "The menu is...incomplete."

This time the cafe shakes so hard that Amelia has to grab onto the table and the still dismayed man who used to be four otters slides off his seat and falls to the floor.

Dave asks me, "Donald, what is Decaf?"

They answer for me, " Decaf is a coffee with the caffeine extracted by some process or other. It was very common."

"About fifteen percent of all coffee consumed," I reluctantly confirm.

A concerned look plastered across his face, Dave says, "Why haven't I heard about it?"

I slide my left hand into my jacket pocket and wrap it around the contents inside. I look up into the smiling face of Nameless and say, "I erased it." while I swing my left hand around as hard as I can in a soaring haymaker punch.

Nameless catches it with ease, holding my left arm out from their head. Their smile grows even wider. They lean in so close those Ruby Red lips are almost on top of mine.

"I'm touching you," They whisper.

I try pulling free, but they hold me in an unbreakable iron grip. I can't even get their arm to move.

"I wonder what amazing thing you have in your hand, Donald?"

Café Muse

Amelia has her hands covering her mouth, the Lady in Red is about six seconds away from orgasm, and Dave is over giving a hand to Otto (what the hell else could a man who used to be four otters have as a name?) helping him to his feet and back to his chair.

They lean in even closer somehow and whisper, "Order it or I will." Then they squeeze my arm until the bones in my left forearm creak. I can literally hear them about to break.

Gritting my teeth and trying to focus through the pain I say, "You can't, you don't know the Menu number."

Their eyes widen, "It's not on the menu!"

I nod fractionally towards the ever-shifting chalkboard

menu behind the counter, each of the thousands of menu options cycling through, appearing, fading, and being replaced by the next set of twenty options as if written and erased by an unseen hand (with exquisite handwriting and an artistic flair).

"It's not on *that* menu," I respond.

They snarl and grind their teeth together audibly.

"Didn't see this coming, did you?"

They search my eyes for deception and find none. Even my indigestion has subsided. "Then you order it."

"No."

"Yes."

"No."

Café Muse

"I'm still holding you, Donald. I thought you cared for Amelia and the others."

Shit.

I hesitate.

"I won't change her, Donald."

I look up into their eyes. We both know the "her" he's talking about. Amelia.

"I'll just erase her. Not gone. Worse than that. Never was. Like you did to Decaf."

Now I get it. They believe that I undid Decaf completely. A Negation. An Erasure from reality itself. No wonder they think this could end reality. Hell, maybe they are right.

"So you think bringing Decaf back to reality will somehow... what?"

"Oh Donald, can you possibly not know this? Anything Erased can never come back. That's the point of me. I'm permanent. Negation is eternal. What is negated cannot exist. Ever. Not in the past, not in the future. That is why you and I are the only two creatures in existence that can even entertain the concept of Decaf. Me because I am master of all things Negated, and you because you somehow, impossibly, negated it."

"But," and here that awful smile came back to those lips, "You can also make anything happen inside this cafe. What a paradox, eh?

"And you and I both know that a paradox can only exist for a tiny instantaneous moment in time before fixing itself."

Café Muse

I despair. "Fixing itself" means exploding and destroying everything, because a paradox cannot exist. Not even for a tiny infinitesimal moment of time. So if one is created despite the impossibility of being created...boom. Universal indigestion.

I swallow. This is going to hurt.

"Amelia?"

I look over to her. She is standing still. Not like a statue. She's as still as the block of marble that might one day be a statue, but not yet...not yet.

"Amelia?" I repeat.

She snaps out of the fear, comes back to life, and answers, "Yes, Donald?"

"I... I need to make an order."

Tears stand unshed in the corners of her eyes as she asks the inevitable question, "What will you have?"

"I'll have..." I swallow hard and look nowhere in shame, "I'll have a Number i."

The Cafe shakes incredibly hard and all of our drinks fall off the tables. The Lady in Red cries out in ecstasy while everyone else calls out in fear as the Cafe Muse experiences its first earthquake. Everyone is holding on to whatever is near to stay upright.

The lights go out entirely and the window beside us cracks, looking for all the universe, like lightning trapped. The emergency lights go on and bathe the scene in an eerie red glow.

Amelia's eyes shed those tears and, as the rumbles subside,

Café Muse

she releases her grip from our table and walks the desolate, eternal, short walk to the counter to get my order.

Another window cracks.

The ceiling suddenly sags about twelve inches over the front entrance.

Otto starts to cry.

Dave is crossing himself (yes, it hurts) and praying (he's Presbyterian, so it doesn't hurt).

The Lady in Red is... oh that's not appropriate at all... I look away quickly.

I look back at Them and see the infinite malice and entirely present glee in those eyes.

My left arm is in agony, still held in place by the crushing grip, fist still clenched tight.

They ask me, "What do you think will happen to reality if the Cafe dies?"

"The Cafe *is* reality," I answer. "That's the whole point, and we both know it."

They smile yet again, "Yes. Yes, it is, and yes we do."

Amelia comes back and sets a plain, white porcelain mug on the table. Inside is an aromatic, black liquid with the faintest sheen of natural coffee bean oils floating on the surface.

A sweet, vicious, bitter, and morning-ruining lie contained in a solution of water and ground beans. Decaf.

"Please don't drink that," I beg.

For an answer, they grab the cup with their free hand.

Café Muse

"Really, don't drink that. I'm trying to save everything, even you."

"I don't want saving, Donald."

I struggle furiously with my left hand and arm, trying to break it free, knowing I won't.

They sigh theatrically (yet again) and then they just...snap the bones in my forearm with barely a grunt of effort.

I scream.

The Cafe screams.

Everyone screams.

Except Them.

They wait until we all settle down and then they ask me, "What's in your hand? What's the heroic last-ditch trick?"

I pant in pain and grind my teeth together long enough to master my tongue, "Don't. Drink. That. Coffee."

Still holding onto my broken arm, they lift the mug to their lips and take a deep draught of the scalding hot lie.

Everyone and everything in the Cafe is frozen into a renaissance-like tableau, waiting on our doom.

And we wait.

And wait.

And wait some more.

Then I smile through the pain

Their eyes are no longer gleeful, they are suspicious. "What is going on? Did you order something besides Decaf? I'll just erase Amelia and we'll do this all over again."

"Nope, that is one hundred percent Decaf anathema. Exactly what you made me order." Then I squeeze my left hand and adjust my fingers as my rapidly swelling broken arm calls out for attention.

Their eyes pin my left hand with their stare.

"What is in your hand?"

I smile.

"What is in your hand!" They scream.

"Let go and I'll show you."

They shake my broken arm viciously and I almost pass out from the pain. My hand opens of its own accord and five small coffee beans fall out onto the table.

Perplexed, they ask, "What the hell is this?"

"Coffea charrieriana."

"What?"

"Coffee that grows without any caffeine. Naturally."

"I don't understand. That's not Decaf. That's just...not-caf. I told you to order Decaf."

"I did."

"I don't understand," they repeat. "Why are we still here? What is happening?"

I pin them with my hardest stare, "Let go of my arm and I'll tell you."

Their eyes narrow in the deepest suspicion yet, but eventually they let go. I recover my broken arm and hold it to my side, trying to stabilize it and reduce the incredible pain shooting up and down my nerves.

After a few breaths to get myself under control in the horrific silence of the cafe, I look around at the cafe and its patrons. The Lady in Red is languidly lounging in a post-coital(solo) glow, her skin mottled with red splotches contrasting horribly with her dress. Otto and Dave are sitting together at Otto's table, two empty shot glasses of espresso picked up off the floor and set in front of each of them.

Amelia has a thoughtful expression on her face and keeps looking into the now empty cup of Decaf and then up to the Ruby Red lips of them. I think she's on the cusp of figuring it out.

Slowly, and with great reluctance I turn my attention back to them and say, "I'm sorry."

Their eyebrows do that thing and they reply, "Beg your pardon?"

"I wish I could, but the deed is done, I can't take it back."

"Take what back?"

I sigh and look down at my broken arm. Then I stretch it out and rest it on the table, whole, unbroken, and pain-free.

"I can't take back the answer."

"What are you talking about?"

"Maths"

"What?"

"Maths."

"Stop wasting time. Tell me what you did. This doesn't change anything...I will destroy all you care about until we get the Decaf!"

"You got the Decaf. That cup was Decaf."

"No, it wasn't!" Decaf can't be real!"

"Maths."

They scream, "Stop saying that!"

"Do you know what you are, really?" I ask them.

"I am Negation!"

"Yet you are part of reality. That is your flaw. You are ultimately nothing more than an irrational expression of universal maths, but you are most definitely real."

"I don't want to be! I want it all to end!"

I look at them with genuine sorrow and sympathy, "I said I was sorry. But you can't end it all. You just don't have that ability. But this was an excellent attempt."

"What did you do?" they cry out in frustration.

"I served you an Imaginary drink."

"I don't understand!"

Amelia gasps and looks at me in horror. She just got it.

She turns to Them with fresh tears and says, "You are...Complex now."

"Maths," I agree solemnly.

"We're not strictly math! We are perception, waveform..." They drift off to stuttering.

"Yes we are," I agree, "and I had five coffee beans in my hand that were naturally decaffeinated, discovered not very long ago. In fact, they were discovered after my...mistake...with decaf. But they presented an interesting train of thought.   If coffee can grow naturally without caffeine, can we take other beans and remove the caffeine on purpose?"

"But you can't," They cry, "that's the whole point! You can't bring decaf back! Paradox!"

I shake my head. "I can't bring it back as it was, you are correct, but maths allows for imagination. Imaginary numbers. Inspiration. And Cafe Muse is where..."

"...Inspiration becomes real," they finish in a daze.

Eventually, they come back to the present from wherever their thoughts took them, and they say,

"So am I just supposed to leave now?"

"I'm afraid that's not possible."

"What? You have not done anything except delay this, Donald. I'm still me and you're still you, and the Cafe is still right here. You might have pulled a fast one, but I'm still going to start breaking your world until you do what I want.

Amelia answers for me, "No, dear. You don't understand. You drank the decaf. You are a Complex composite now, part of you is imaginary. Maths. If you leave the boundary of the Cafe, you will be a paradox. A square root of a negative number. You will cease to exist.

They look up at me sharply. "You did this to me?"

Café Muse

"I did this for you."

"For me?"

"You don't really want to destroy reality, do you?"

"Of course I do! I've been trying for eternity!"

"Why?"

"So I can cease to exist! I am tired. I want to go!"

I lift my hand and point at the Cafe door. "So go."

They abruptly sit up rigid in their seat and their head snaps around to look at the front doors.

After a short eternity, they turn back to me with emotions warring all over their face.

"Really?"

"Yes."

"And I'll be gone. Forever?"

"Forever. Eternal rest."

They stare at me for a few seconds that eventually stretch into a minute.

"Will it hurt?"

"I hope not."

"You don't know?"

"I don't. I'm sorry."

They rise from the table and say, "Stand up, Donald."

I stand.

They come around the table and wrap me in a huge hug that scares the crap out of me before I realize it's in gratitude. They begin to sob openly repeating softly, "Thank you. Thank you. Thank you."

Café Muse

They walk to the door as I head over to Otto and whisper in his ear. He shakes his head in the negative. I guess he's happy as a man disguised as an otter now. He doesn't want to be changed back.

At the door, They turn around and look at all of us. They don't say anything, but we all nod to them anyway.

They shove the bent and semi-jammed door open, walk out onto the sidewalk, and turn up the street and out of sight. A few seconds later we hear a loud pop and woosh of air as if rushing to fill a sudden void where a tortured creature had once stood.

I feel a light hand on my shoulder and I turn to see Amelia standing next to me. "That was a good thing you did, Donald. That poor creature..." She stops and removes her hand, walking away to the counter on the other side of the universe.

Before she gets there, she turns around and says, "Part-time."

"What?"

"I'm only a part-time angel."

I smile, "What are you the rest of the time?"

A spark of joy fires up behind those green eyes, "Well, I'm a barista at Café Muse, of course."

"Of course."

DANIEL NICK
WAR
DOG
HOUND OF THE GODS BOOK ONE

Drustan Seta is not a hero. He's never been anything other than a War Dog – a violent solution to other people's problems. A shooter with a knack for hitting his target. But then he butchered the wrong person, and Dru was kicked out of a military branch filled with humans, cryptids, and a few other creatures from myths and legends known as Extras.

Now, Dru is alone again. Alone, that is, until the wife of the only man he had been willing to call family knocks on his door asking for help. Her husband is gone, maybe dead, and there's a nasty group called Broadhead Securities mixed up in his disappearance.

Dru sets out to either rescue the closest thing to a family he's had in forever, or kill every last person involved in his death, only to discover devastating secrets, international conspiracies, and a plan to bring back the Old Gods. But Dru has secrets of his own and a trauma-filled past that has shaped him into the guy who can do what the Heroes can't, and now he has one shot to teach them just how loyal a War Dog can be when you mess with family.

The Ace of Cups

By JJ Caler

Copyright © 2024 J.J. Caler

Written by J.J. Caler

All rights reserved.

Published by JJ Caler Publishing

A SHORT STORY BY
JJ CALER
THE ACE OF CUPS

The Prelude

In a world where reality and dreams intertwine, where the mundane meets the magical, there exists a place just off the beaten path. A place where fate is sealed with a single card, and destiny is written in the stars.

Ellis, a struggling artist, finds himself on an unexpected journey. A broken fan belt leads him to a tiny mountain town, where a chance encounter with a mysterious woman named Laurie changes everything. In her dimly lit shop, amidst the scent of herbs and old books, Ellis draws a card – the Ace of Cups.

"This card," Laurie whispers, "holds the key to your journey. It represents the beginning of something profound, a wellspring of emotions and possibilities."

As the card drifts from her hand to the worn wooden tabletop, Ellis's story begins. A tale of love, magic, and the supernatural, where every choice leads to a new path, and every path holds a secret waiting to be uncovered.

Welcome to "The Ace of Cups."

The Ace of Cups

The Shop

Ellis had been driving for hours,
the California sun beating down

relentlessly. He was on his way to a gallery meeting, a chance to finally showcase his work. Ever since meeting Awvie, his luck seemed to be turning around. But today was different. The fan belt of his '68 Chevelle had snapped, leaving him stranded in a tiny mountain town.

The mechanic shook his head sympathetically. "It'll be a while. We need to ship the part in. Not many '68 Chevelles with heart transplants like yours come through here."

Reluctantly, Ellis left his beloved car and wandered down the parched street. A sign swinging in the breeze caught his eye: "Coffee and Crystals." He didn't need a crystal, but the promise of coffee was too tempting to resist.

Ellis stepped into the dimly lit shop, the scent of herbs and old books filling the air. Laurie, the witch, sat behind a small wooden table, her eyes twinkling with mischief.

"Pick a card and a gemstone," Laurie said, spreading a deck of tarot cards across the table.

Ellis hesitated, then reached out touching the smoothest of the stones she had laid out, and then drew a card. The Ace of Cups. Laurie smiled knowingly.

"You picked my favorite out of the stones I had laid out! I use this one a lot for grounding myself, and to help me rid myself of negativity. I often hold it to help clear my energy. I have a gold sheen obsidian mirror as well."

Ellis looked at the card, feeling a strange connection to it.

"What does this mean for me?" he asked.

Laurie leaned in, her voice soft and enigmatic. "Ahh, the Ace of Cups. An opportunity for an emotional experience or growth. New feelings. Spirituality. Intuition. You are in tune and unbothered. Truly in the flow. In addition to that though, I noticed how the bird was bringing something to the cat. If you follow your intuition, life will bring you what you need. Work with the Universe, and it will work with you."

"The universe has been acting tricky, but I am letting it flow. It seems like it has a plan... I hope it aligns with mine... I need that shack near the beach," Ellis replied, with humor in his voice, but something she said intrigued him. "I need to know more about this bird and cat..."

Laurie chuckled softly. "The cat is just laying there! The cup and the bird are doing the work."

The Train

Meet Ellis... I would describe him for you, but he is a bit of a mystery. He was just a tall man in a long black overcoat, sitting in a private car on a crowded train. He was facing toward the front and looking to the side, out the window, watching the wolves run in the fields. They were a real portrait against the backdrop of the snow-peaked mountains.

The dining car was a carefully designed mix of old-world charm and modern convenience. There were gleaming mahogany tables with intricate carvings, plush velvet seats in deep burgundy with patterns of small vines and orange and yellow flowers, and art deco light fixtures casting a warm, golden glow throughout the cabin. The clinking of silverware and the murmur of conversations added to the ambiance, creating a sense of timeless elegance.

Ellis wasn't sure where he was going. He just got an envelope with a small note inside. *"Meet me on the train..."* and at this time. Ellis looked around at his life, and decided, why the hell not. Nothing here was going to change with or without him. Let's go meet a stranger on a train.

He got together a small suitcase and left his house, drove a hundred and twenty miles, and got onto a train. He has been on it for days now. He was still waiting for her, but he wasn't missing the world around him... this time. For once, he wasn't the one at the wheel. He could really enjoy the landscape, changes in weather, wildlife that was all going by. Every morning was like a new adventure outside those glass panes, calling to him. Come outside, Ellis. Live.

Ellis ran his fingers over the small object in his hand which he held beneath the table, carefully keeping it out of view. "This could change everything," he thought to himself.

His mind drifted back to the mountains of eastern California. He remembered driving up a winding mountain road, the air had the taste of smoke but the sky was clear. The scent of pine trees filled the car as he turned onto the dry, unpaved road, a trail of dust rising behind him. He arrived at a secluded cabin surrounded by towering pines.

Laurie greeted him with a warm hug. Today would be another first for the two of them. She had a calming presence, yet a mysterious vibe surrounded her, accentuated by the small, intricate amulet she always wore around her neck.

"I am so excited, I am glad you called on me, Ellis." She was beaming with exuberance, then she paused, "Are you sure, though? We can't take it back. Not any of it. When it is done, it is done."

He only paused for a moment, a last thought on the price of things. "Yes, I am positive. I have to do this."

"Bring it with you." She pointed to the bag on his car seat then led Ellis down a well-worn path between the trees, "Do you still have the card?"

"Always," Ellis smiled. "I have carried it with me since that first day."

"She's right, you know."

Ellis furrowed his brow, "About what?"

"You're a weirdo. You would make such a good familiar." She turned toward him, her eyes twinkling with mischief. "I could make you a nice white opossum, or, I could always use another raccoon."

"Yeah, opossums aren't very good painters, and I see how it worked out for that other raccoon of yours. Obsessed with the landfill... Not that I don't mind a good junk scrounge." Ellis grinned, "But I think I had better pass."

They stepped out into a clearing near a lake where her friends were gathered.

The air was thick with the scent of herbs and the sound of the forest at night.

They were preparing for his arrival, mixing ingredients and

setting up a small fire. The atmosphere was charged with anticipation. Laurie reassured Ellis that this would help him and Awvie see things clearly.

They began chanting lyrics softly, their voices blending with the sounds of the forest. The fire crackled, and the full moon cast an ethereal glow over the scene. Ellis watched in awe as Laurie and the others performed. He opened his bag and handed her a large folder and kneeled next to the fire.

"Don't worry, Ellis. This will work."

"Famous last words," he whispered to himself.

For months, he had let himself become more and more attached to Awvie. She was young and beautiful, and had a heart filled with kindness. And for months he watched her struggles grow more intense from a distance... with his hands tied. Sometimes trying to help only resulted in her pushing back.

"You think I am a broken little girl and you want to save me." she said. "Well I am not. I am tougher than most. You don't understand everything."

"I know you aren't a child. You are intelligent and clever and a strong, beautiful woman," he answered, feeling the pain inside his heart. He couldn't see her eyes, couldn't read her intentions.

"I could hurt you. I could put my foot on your throat and crush you." she warned.

"I know. You could hurt me in so many ways. But you haven't. Just choose not to. You don't have any reason to."

She could hurt him. He felt the pain often and hid it from her. Maybe there was more truth to what she said than he cared to admit. Maybe this was a mistake. But he had to try to let her know, they had a choice. That there was something special here, and they shouldn't let it slip through their hands. This seemed like the only way, and besides, it was too late.

She carried so much, her work and life at home. He saw her at the edge of breaking, and pulling herself up again. He wanted to take her away from the struggle and set her free. Let her be who she really was. The complete her. And he wanted to love her and show her that she could love.

The Girl

Awvie stood quietly in the door watching him, still trying to decide whether he was the right stranger on this train. Her stranger. She could just make out the color of his dark brown eyes from the side. His features showed a lifetime of change. He probably had many years that he was in better shape physically than he was now, but he wasn't particularly heavy. His hair had lost all traces of its original color. There were small scars on his hands that swore to his lifetime of labor.

A voice inside was telling her, 'Just step through the door, Awvie. There is no judgment here. He will let you be yourself and tell your story.'

Ellis had been looking at her reflection for some time. The muse that had inspired this adventure for him. She stood tall and still against the threshold of the door. She had blonde hair with light purple highlights and silvery eyes. She felt familiar to him. Like someone he should know, someone he was connected to... maybe in another lifetime. Characters from another story that were never given their ending. A story unfinished.

"Come inside with me, Awvie," he said gently without looking back at her. "We'll be safe here. Tell me the stories that keep you awake at night."

He had been losing a little ground the night before. Ellis had begun passing the time drawing while he waited for her to arrive. Just the thought of this mystery girl gave him reams of portraits in his mind. But the character in this image arrived in a winter forest and he wasn't sure where he was going anymore. Something was still missing.

Now he was getting the visions again, and he wasn't even awake. In fact, his head was slightly pounding. Strong perfumes from one of the doors down the corridor being left open. But his eyes were still clear. "I hope you don't mind if I tell you," he began, with a smile growing across his lips, "You are incredibly beautiful today."

The silence was deafening as he waited for her response. She seemed to be lost in another place, maybe another world where she was about to turn and walk in the other direction. Ellis wished he could reach into that world and pull her through, but he had to wait for her to step through on her own.

In a small attempt to get her attention, he picked up a small porcelain pitcher with a blue floral design on it and poured thick cream over a small bowl of fresh strawberries. "They are the best," he grinned, "I could eat these by the truckload, couldn't you?"

"We shouldn't be here." she almost whispered, a slight tremble in her voice.

"My mind says, where else would we be? But my heart says I am glad we are both here." he slid the strawberries away, knowing she had no taste for them. "Please, sit with me. We should do this. We should both know."

"We probably shouldn't," she remarked as she slid into the seat across from him.

A server stopped at the table and offered coffee, which both accepted without any argument. After she left, Ellis looked at Awvie, "We both have said, there were things going on in the universe that brought us together. We both should have left. But we didn't. It is like causality. One action causes a reaction and it continues out like ripples on a pond, from the beginning of time until the moment you said to me, 'we should stop this'."

Awvie just looked back across the table without saying anything. She knew what he was talking about. All the strange coincidences that made them see each other.

"I made a choice that day. I thought about it. Then I covered up everything before, and opened a new door with you. It wasn't the realization of what I felt for you, but that you felt it too." Ellis looked down at his hands, holding the warm cup, "We snared each other, you know. It wasn't just you."

"You still don't want to believe me. I told you so much. I told you that... it doesn't matter. We are both here. What is it you needed to show me?" Her frustration was clear.

"You know all of the scenes I tried to paint for you. All of the places I imagined for us. The lives we could live," he lifted the small trinket in his hand and showed it to her.

There were interlacing rings of silver that spun around each other and in the center a small gem, glowing like it was on fire. There were tiny green bands like vines that wove themselves around it and up into a chain that acted as a necklace.

"Laurie and her friends made this for us."

"It's pretty," she said with a smile. "What do you mean, for us? What is it?"

"It is possibilities for the impossible." he answered with a serious note in his tone. "It can take us there. You... We can see the choices. But only so far."

"Why did Laurie make it?" Awvie asked, her curiosity piqued.

Ellis took a deep breath, knowing this was the moment to reveal the truth. "Laurie and her friends... They are witches. I know it sounds unbelievable, but they have powers, real powers. I went to her for help when I felt you slipping away. I didn't want a simple love potion. I wanted our love to be real and organic. But I needed something special, something that could show us the possibilities."

Awvie's eyes widened, a mix of disbelief and intrigue. "Witches? And you believe in this?"

"I didn't at first," Ellis admitted. "But one night, Laurie

read a card for me, just one card from a Tarot deck, and she used words that were often in our conversations. It struck a nerve. We became friends after that, and she and her friends helped me grow my business with the galleries. When things got dire for the two of us, I asked for their help again. They made this amulet for us, a powerful trinket that can show us the lives we could have."

Awvie looked at the amulet, her mind racing with thoughts and emotions. "So, this can show us the choices we have?"

"Yes," Ellis said, his voice filled with hope. "It can show us the possibilities, the lives we could live together. But only if you are willing to see them."

The Town

Ellis glanced out the window, his eyes catching sight of an old, abandoned ghost town in the distance. The dilapidated buildings stood frozen in a forgotten past, their weathered boards creaking in the gentle breeze. Sagebrush and tumbleweeds dotted the landscape, adding to the desolate atmosphere. The remnants of an old mining town, once bustling with life and activity, now lay in ruins, shrouded in a haunting silence.

The morning sun seemed to highlight the crumbling structures, with their faded paint and broken windows. An old saloon, its sign barely legible, leaned precariously to one side. The general store, with its door hanging off its hinges. Rusted mining equipment lay scattered around, half-buried in the dirt.

"Look," Ellis said, pointing out the window. "Do you see that ghost town?"

Awvie turned her head, her curiosity piqued. "Yes, I see it. Why?"

Ellis took a deep breath, his mind racing with the possibilities. "We need to get off at the next stop. That place... it's perfect. It's secluded, and no one will disturb us there. We can use the amulet safely."

Awvie's eyes widened, filled with excitement and apprehension. "Are you sure?"

"Don't worry, Ellis. This will work." Laurie said as she loosened her robe.

The Ace of Cups

There were no silly pointed hats like in childhood stories. No one was dressed for Halloween. But the robes were real. Theirs were made from very thin suede. Almost like a fabric. There were stars and moons on hers, as if they had been tattooed into the hide. He caught a glimpse of her bare flesh hiding beneath as she held out her hand to him.

"Take off your jacket and shirt, Ellis, and bring the items I asked you for."

He drew a long breath and removed the shirt and jacket, then picked up the bag and followed her to the fire. Her friends were still reciting the lyrics to some forgotten song and Laurie motioned for him to kneel by the fire.

Ellis felt the rough texture of his leather pants against his skin, almost chafing in the summer heat. The pants were made from the same thin suede as the witches' robes, a necessity to avoid interfering with the spell. He shifted uneasily, the leather clinging to him in the heat of the fire. As the ritual progressed, the witches began to shed their robes, revealing more of their bare flesh, emphasizing the natural connection required for their magic.

"Ellis, this is important. You have to be absolutely positive the two of you are alone when you do this. Anyone else near you and things will get messy. Spirits can get lost, and trapped in the wrong place, wrong person." She locked her gaze on his, something like caring in her eyes, "And for the love of Cate, don't be near a graveyard... Are you sure that you love her?"

"Yes. More than anything." Ellis answered and opened the bag he carried with him.

"She has to choose, this won't affect her judgment..."

"Yes," Ellis replied, his voice steady. "It's the best place. Trust me."

Awvie nodded, her curiosity overcoming her hesitation. "Alright, let's do it."

As the train approached the next stop, Ellis felt a sense of determination wash over him. It would all be over soon.

The train came to a halt at the small, dusty station. Ellis and Awvie quickly disembarked, their footsteps echoing on the wooden platform. The station was nearly deserted, with only a few travelers milling about.

Ellis spotted a small car rental kiosk near the entrance. "Let's rent a car," he suggested, leading Awvie towards the kiosk. The attendant, a middle-aged man with a friendly smile, greeted them.

"Good morning! How can I help you today?" the attendant asked.

"We'd like to rent a car," Ellis replied. "Something reliable that can handle a bit of rough terrain."

The attendant nodded and handed them a form to fill out. "We have a few options. How about a sturdy SUV? It's perfect for exploring off-the-beaten-path places."

"That sounds great," Ellis agreed, quickly filling out the necessary paperwork. Within minutes, they were handed the keys to a rugged SUV.

They loaded their belongings into the car and set off towards the ghost town. The road was winding and narrow, flanked by tall pine trees and rocky outcrops. As they drove, the landscape gradually transformed, becoming more arid and desolate.

Ellis parked the car at the edge of the town, and they stepped out, taking in the eerie silence.

"This is it," Ellis said, his voice filled with determination. "Let's find a spot where we can use the amulet."

Awvie nodded, her curiosity and excitement growing with each step. Together, they ventured into the heart of the ghost town.

Ellis took Awvie's left hand, his touch gentle yet firm. "I have never asked you to choose. I could never give you an ultimatum. I just want you to know the options. This amulet," he said, his voice filled with emotion, "can show us the lives we could have together. But it's not without risks."

Awvie looked into his eyes, her curiosity and apprehension mingling. "What kind of risks?"

Ellis's mind flashed back to Laurie's warnings. *"Spirits can get lost, and trapped in the wrong place, wrong person,"* her voice echoed in his memory. He took a deep breath and repeated the warning for Awvie. "We have to be absolutely sure we're alone when we do this. And... we mustn't be near a graveyard."

Awvie nodded, her grip on his hand tightening. "I trust you, Ellis. I've always trusted you, and I still don't know why."

The Witch

Laurie turned to him, her eyes serious. "Ellis, this amulet requires a sacrifice. Something precious to you. It must be given willingly."

Ellis opened the bag, revealing a wooden case that contained a brush set, given to him by his mother before she passed away. And a large bundle tied with orange yarn, stuffed with paintings. All of the paintings he had made for Awvie. Her portraits, the places he imagined for them, his book of dreams.

"These," he said, his voice trembling. "These are precious to me."

He hesitated for a moment, then reached into his pocket and pulled out a card. The Ace of Cups. He looked at it, the image of the overflowing chalice symbolizing love and emotional fulfillment. There was a cat, laying at its base and a small bird in flight above it. Letting his breath escape slowly, he placed the card on top of the bundle and held it out to Laurie.

Laurie's expression changed slightly, a cringe flickering across her face as she pulled her hands away. "No, not that. You need to keep that."

Ellis nodded, understanding the significance of the card. He tucked it back into his pocket.

Laurie took the other items gently, her expression softening. "Thank you, Ellis. Your sacrifice will not be in vain."

One of Laurie's friends reached into the fire with her bare hands and pulled what looked like a necklace from the coals. It was glowing bright orange, yet she seemed unbothered by the blazing heat of the metal.

Laurie and the others, now bare beneath the moonlight, lifted their arms toward the sky. She said something he couldn't translate, and a large ball of flame appeared above them, hovering over the center of the fire. The one holding the amulet stepped behind Ellis and held the necklace open above his head.

The witches' chanting grew louder, and his sketchbook, collection of paintings and brushes were placed into the fire. The flames danced higher, and the amulet began to glow with an otherworldly light. Ellis felt a strange energy coursing through him, a sense of connection to something greater.

The ritual reached its climax, and the amulet was completed. Laurie held it up to

Ellis, her eyes filled with both hope and sorrow. "Ellis, it will show everything. Some things you won't want to see... Some things she won't want to see."

He reached to take it from her hands and she jerked away.

"No, don't. We can't touch this together. I will show you how to use it, then you pick it up when I set it down." She made sure he understood how to wrap the chain on both of their wrists then laid it at his feet. "Ellis... I hope this works out for you. Both of you. I can't be involved in anything else between the two of you now. I mean, we will always be friends, but not potions or hexes or anything. Your relationship with each other is out of bounds for all of us here."

The Hotel

They found a secluded spot in the old hotel. The lobby was like taking a step into an old western movie, with its high ceilings and ornate wooden fixtures. Dust coated every surface, muting the once-rich colors of the faded wallpaper and the dark wood paneling. A grand chandelier hung from the ceiling, its crystals dulled by years of neglect. The air was thick with the scent of aged leather and old wood, mingling with the faint aroma of dust.

Ellis held the amulet between them, its surface glinting in the dim light that filtered through the dusty windows. "Are you ready?" he asked.

Awvie took a deep breath, her eyes filled with determination. "Yes."

Ellis wrapped the chain around their wrists, their left hands held together, he ran his thumb across her fingers. As he activated the amulet, a shimmering light enveloped them. The world around them faded, replaced by vivid visions of their future.

They saw themselves together, living a life of happiness and love. He took her to all the places they had talked about. He built her the small home in the hills, with her own craft room, just as he had described it to her. He spent hours sitting on the patio, watching her making pottery and writing stories, while she watched him painting dreams on his canvas.

Their lives were filled with passion and it lasted, unblemished, for twenty years. But then, Ellis fell ill, and Awvie was left alone, her heart shattered.

The vision shifted, showing Awvie's other choice. She saw herself returning to her old life, filled with the struggles of a mundane existence. Her husband was there, but the deep connection she shared with Ellis was absent.

Her career was her life. Everything was so perfectly practical. And then there were the punctuations where things didn't go smoothly. A job choice that didn't work out. Moving from one place to the next and restarting again. That one account on her phone she had refused to open for years, laying silent. Probably empty now. No one on the other side.

Tears welled up in Awvie's eyes as the visions faded. She looked down at the wedding ring on her finger and then at Ellis, her heart torn between the two paths. The weight of the decision pressed down on her, and she knew that the choice she made now would shape the rest of her life.

Ellis, it will show everything. Some things you won't want to see... Some things she won't want to see."

He could still hear Laurie's voice as he reached out, gently taking Awvie's hand. "Whatever you decide, I'll be here," he said softly.

Awvie glanced back at the ghost town, the morning sun casting long shadows over the crumbling buildings. Ellis's words echoed in her mind: *"Spirits can get lost, and trapped in the wrong place, or wrong person."*

Her chest physically shuddered as she exhaled, her gaze returning to Ellis. "Let's see where this takes us," she whispered, her voice filled with a mix of hope and uncertainty.

As they walked back toward the rental car, a gentle breeze picked up. A small card slipped from Ellis's pocket, drifting away in the wind. It landed face up on the ground, the image of a chalice overflowing with water, new beginnings and emotional fulfillment. The card lay there, a silent witness to the journey Ellis and Awvie shared that day. **The Ace of Cups.**

Jasper and the
Salamander
J. J. Caler

Erin
Rise
J. J. Caler

The Witch at the
World's End
J. J. Caler